Grover

Horace

Ida

Joshua

JE BO
(A,B,C)

Kirby

Leroy

AN ANNOYING ABC

Olivia

Petunia

Quentin

Stella

Nigel

Roland

Tod

by Barbara Bottner • illustrated by Michael Emberley

Alfred A. Knopf ⚘ New York

Ursula Vera Winthrop X Y Z Yves Miss Mabel Xavier Zelda

It was a quiet morning until . . .

Adelaide annoyed Bailey.

Bailey blamed Clyde.

Clyde cried.

Dexter drooled on Eloise.

Eloise elbowed Flora.

Flora fumed.

Grover grabbed Horace,

who howled at Ida,

which irritated Joshua, who jabbed Kirby.

Kirby kicked Leroy.

Leroy completely lost it . . .

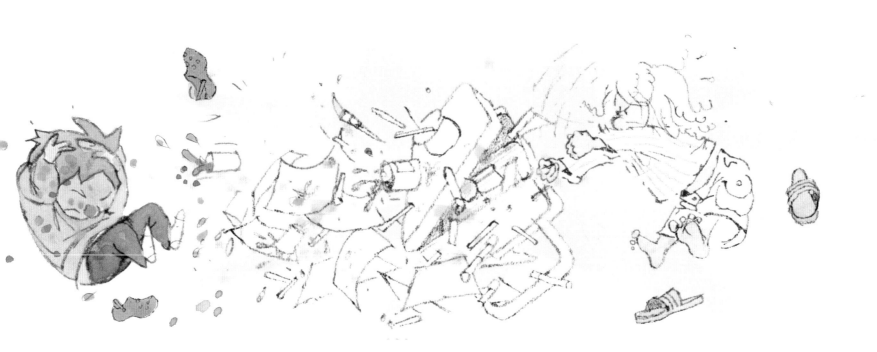

and then lied to Miss Mabel.

"My, my, *my*!" muttered Miss Mabel.

Nigel nudged Olivia.

Olivia overreacted.

Petunia pestered Quentin.

Quentin quarreled with Roland.

Roland rumbled,

Stella stumbled,

Todd tumbled,

and upended
Ursula.

Winthrop wept!

Vera vocalized!

Xavier exploded!

Yves yelled!

And then . . .

Zelda zapped Adelaide.

Astonishing!

"Zelda?"

"Adelaide started it!"

But then . . .

Adelaide apologized.

Everyone apologized.

And then

Adelaide, Bailey, Clyde, Dexter, Eloise,
Flora, Grover, Horace, Ida, Joshua, Kirby,

Leroy, Miss Mabel, Nigel, Olivia, Petunia, Quentin, Roland, Stella, Todd, Ursula, Vera, Winthrop, Xavier, Yves, and Zelda . . .

had a quiet afternoon . . .

mostly.

THIS IS A BORZOI BOOK PUBLISHED BY ALFRED A. KNOPF

Text copyright © 2011 by Barbara Bottner
Illustrations copyright © 2011 by Bird Productions, Inc.

Visit us on the Web! www.randomhouse.com/kids

Educators and librarians, for a variety of teaching tools, visit us at
www.randomhouse.com/teachers

Library of Congress Cataloging-in-Publication Data
Bottner, Barbara.
An annoying ABC / by Barbara Bottner ; illustrated by Michael Emberley. — 1st ed.
p. cm.
Summary: When Adelaide annoys Bailey, their entire preschool class gets upset,
one child after another, until Zelda zaps Adelaide and a round of apologies begins.
ISBN 978-0-375-86708-8 (trade) — ISBN 978-0-375-96708-5 (lib. bdg.)
[1. Behavior—Fiction. 2. Nursery schools—Fiction. 3. Schools—Fiction. 4. Alphabet.] I. Emberley, Michael, ill. II. Title.
PZ7.B6586Ann 2011 [E]—dc22 2011011843

The illustrations in this book were drawn in 2B mechanical pencil and painted with
tube watercolor on 90-pound Arches hot press paper on two continents!

MANUFACTURED IN CHINA
September 2011
10   9   8   7   6   5   4   3   2   1

First Edition